A POWER FAMILIES ADVENTURE

For Lilu - S.M.
For Drew - A.E.

Meet Max and Haggis at the Power Families website – www.powerfamilies.com

First published in Great Britain in 2006 by Jack Hook Ltd.
Whithurst Lodge, Kirdford, West Sussex RH14 0JX
www.jackhook.com

ISBN 0-9554296-1-7
ISBN 978-0-9554296-1-3

1 3 5 7 9 10 8 6 4 2

A CIP catalogue record for this book is available from the British Library.

Printed in Belgium by Proost.

A POWER FAMILIES™ Adventure

Story by
SUSE MOORE

Illustrated by
ANDY ELKERTON

Jackhook™

Outside the old windmill on the top of Power Hill, Max and Haggis were rolling snowballs.

"Watch me, Haggis.
I am Max the Juggler!" said Max, throwing two fluffy snowballs up into the air.

Suddenly he caught sight of something sparkling like a diamond on the sea below.

"Yippee! The Nippy Knot's here," he cried, spying a tall, silver sail. "Let's..."

both snowballs landed on his head.

"...go, Haggis!" he spluttered.

Max and Haggis raced through
the wind-fields on Max's snowboard.
They weaved in and out of the turbines
that were making electricity
for Glen Boggle.

SWISH! SWOOSH!
through the snow they swooped like a rocket.

"Hang on, Haggis!" shouted Max,
aiming the snowboard at a hump.
"We're going to catch some air!"

the snowboard took off...

THUMP! BUMP! they crashed into a pile of snow on the jetty, right next to where the Nippy Knot had landed.
"Ahoy, Max!" waved Grandpa Power from the deck.
"I've crossed the seas tae see yer circus show. Are ye sure ye're up for it?"
"I am," said Max, brushing off the snow.
"We've been practising for weeks at school. The Solly Circus has just arrived in Glen Boggle and they're putting up a huge stripy tent for us."

Grandpa looked up at the wind turbines and raised a bushy eyebrow. "I dinnae like the way those blades are turning so slowly. We'll need tae make the wind blow harder tae make enough electricity tae keep that big tent nice and warm inside.

"Solly Circus have their own power generator so they can make their own electricity. Anyway, no-one can actually make the wind blow harder," laughed Max. Grandpa's eyes twinkled.

"True. The wind is its own master but a bit of persuasion sometimes works a treat.

Now let's go tae the windmill. I'm a bit peckish for some Power's porridge."

Grandpa Power sat in front of a steaming bowl of porridge inside the higgeldy-piggeldy, creaking wood kitchen.

"I am Max the Juggler," announced Max, throwing two of his Dad's golf balls up into the air. He caught one but the other bounced off the ceiling with a PING!

PLOP! the ball landed in Grandpa's porridge. Max turned as red as his hair. "Ach, Max. Ye need tae practise a wee bit more laddie," said Grandpa, just as Max's Dad walked in.

"There's no need," said his Dad. "The Solly Circus power generator has broken down.

Tomorrow's circus show is cancelled."

My house
WIND FARMERS WEEKLY
Haggis
Max
HAGGIS

"What do you mean the show's cancelled?" exclaimed Max.
"We can't plug the Big Top into the village's electricity supply because everyone else needs it." said his Dad.

"Your school,

your friends' homes,

Scotty's shop,

and Glamclash Weavers all need to keep warm."

Max's heart sank like a stone.

"It's not fair!" he said. "Everyone in Glen Boggle is coming to our show."

"Max, I'm sorry," said his Dad. "But unless the wind blows harder we can't make more electricity."

Max snatched the porridge-covered golf ball from Grandpa's bowl and ran up the stairs to his bedroom.

Max sat on his bed staring glumly at the golf ball in his hand.
"Max, my laddie, I've got a wee idea that might get the wind tae blow,"
whispered Grandpa, popping his head around the door.
"Will ye come down tae the Nippy Knot with me?"

"No one can boss the wind about," mumbled Max.
"True, but I have an idea that might persuade it tae blow,"
said Grandpa, with a twinkle in his eye.
"Will ye give it a wee try?"

Tangled cables and humming computers sat piled up to the roof of the Nippy Knot's cabin.
"We need tae find my old tin box," said Grandpa, looking around scratching his head.
Max climbed into the tangle of snaky cables and started digging around.
Suddenly he felt something flat and smooth underneath a roll of wire.

"Is this it Grandpa?" he asked, pulling out a shiny metal box.
"Ach, ye clever laddie, it is! Let's take a look inside."

2344 24 =22 21=191 583
239400 0853 97 83 30212
1902385803475985
2291̇4u890124
58902-078957892--
2394820-1089577511
01289474 2729i34892
33733-276

"Here ye are! This should get the wind tae blow," said Grandpa, handing Max a crumpled piece of paper.

" 'Power's Bagpipe Blowing Tune'– to be played at sunset at the top o' Spike Hill," read Max.

"Ye'll need these too," said Grandpa, unhooking a dusty set of bagpipes from the wall.

"But mind ye hurry up Spike Hill, the sun's about tae set."

"A tune will get the wind to blow?" asked Max.
"That's why I gave ye the
bagpipe lessons, laddie,"
said Grandpa, with a
chuckle.

Max and Haggis reached the top of Spike Hill just as the sun came to rest on the sea like a big, glowing orange.

Max pulled the Blowing Tune out of his pocket, put the bagpipes under his arm and blew into the blowpipe.

POOF! A cloud of dust flew off the bag.

"Atchoo!" sneezed Haggis.

Rowahhhhhhhh!

grumbled the bagpipes.

Max blew up the bag again.

Blahruuuuuuuuuuuuuuuuuuh! rattled the pipes, like a rickety car horn.

Haggis put her paws over her ears.

Max tried again.

Rowahhhhhhhhh!

Blahruuuuuuuuuuuuh!

And again.

Rowahhhhhhhh!

BLARUUUUUUUUUUUUUUH!

"That's it!" said Max, throwing down the bagpipes.

"I'll never conjure up the wind and I'll never be a juggler!"

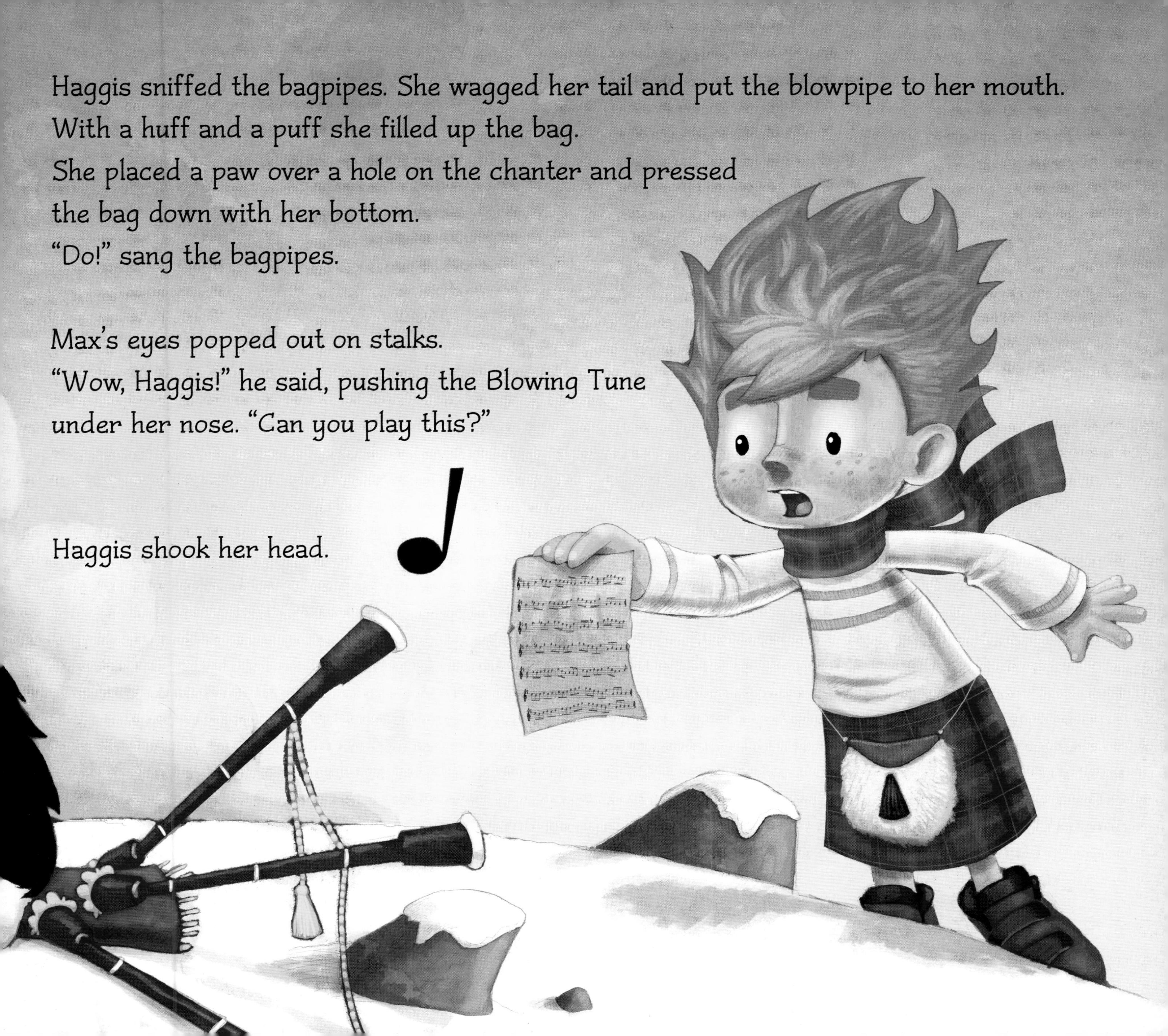

Haggis sniffed the bagpipes. She wagged her tail and put the blowpipe to her mouth.
With a huff and a puff she filled up the bag.
She placed a paw over a hole on the chanter and pressed the bag down with her bottom.
"Do!" sang the bagpipes.

Max's eyes popped out on stalks.
"Wow, Haggis!" he said, pushing the Blowing Tune under her nose. "Can you play this?"

Haggis shook her head.

Max looked at the sun. It was only half an orange now.
"I know, we can play it together!" he said.
"Woof!" said Haggis, blowing up the bag.
She pressed it down with her bottom at the same time as Max played the Blowing Tune on the chanter.

'Do-do-re-do-do-la!'
sang the bagpipes

'WOOSH!' replied the wind, whistling in over the sea, roaring up the hills towards the music.

The blades of the wind turbines started spinning faster and faster.
'La-la-me-la-la-la-me!' sang the bagpipes.
The wind howled and snatched at the Blowing Tune and bagpipes.
"No!" cried Max, leaping up.

He caught the bagpipes in one hand and the tune in the other.
But suddenly the wind turned into a whirlwind and scooped up Max and Haggis.

Round and round it spun them
like a huge hamster wheel.

The blades of the wind turbines accelerated,
generating more and more electricity.

All of a sudden the whirwind
spun off the top of the hill.

"Help!" cried Max. "We're being blown out to sea!"

But when the whirlwind reached the Nippy Knot it unfurled, landing Max and Haggis squarely on the deck of the boat.

“Phew!” said Max, his head spinning.

“Ach, ye and Haggis did a grand job conjuring up that wind! There’s going tae be plenty of electricity for Solly’s Big Top now,” said Grandpa, chuckling.

And the very next evening...

In the brightly-lit, toasty-warm Big Top
Max juggled three golf balls at once.
The audience cheered.
"Woof! Woof!" barked Haggis.

"That's my grandson!" shouted Grandpa.
"The windmaker and the juggler!"

THE END.

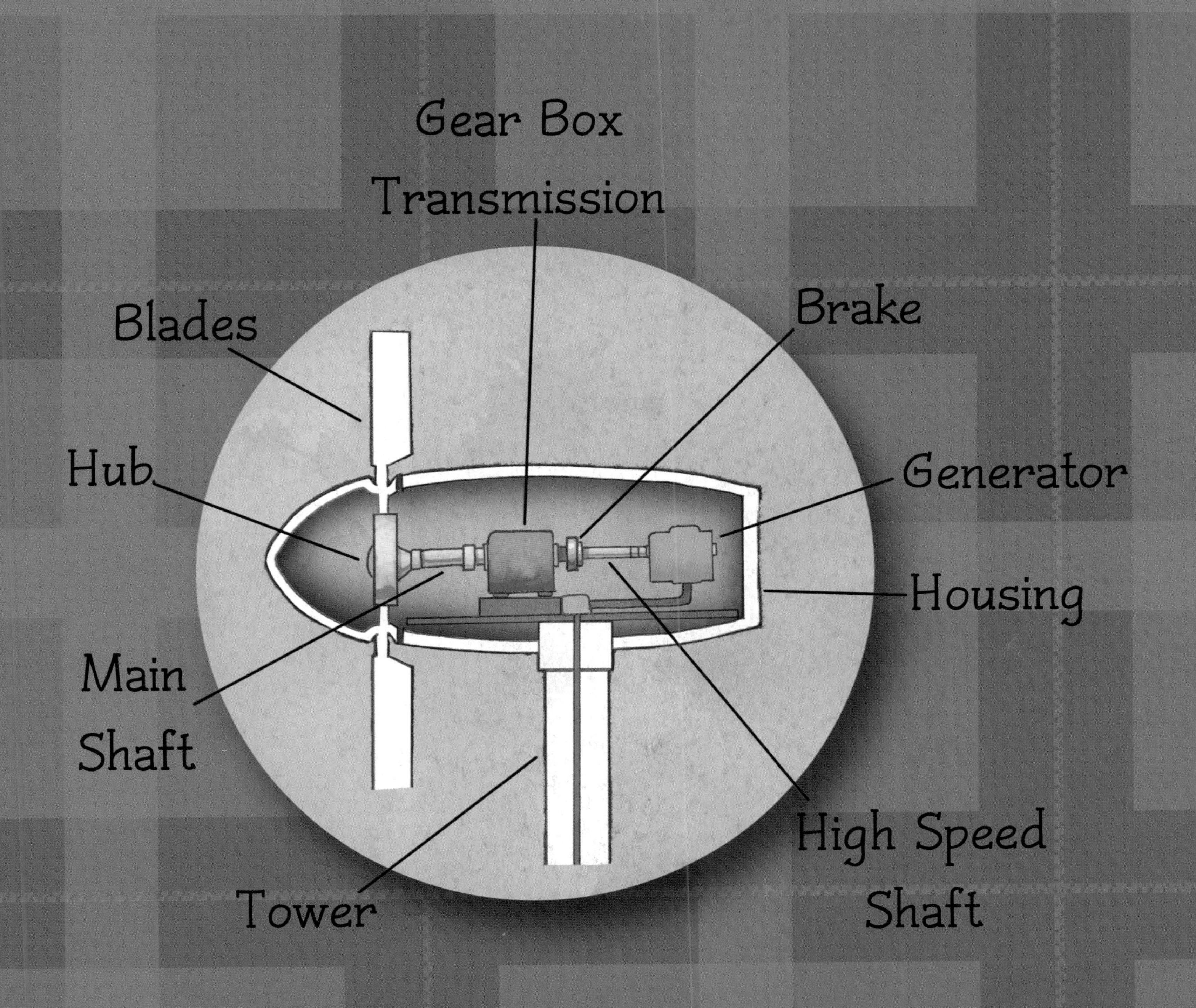

The Inner Workings of a Wind Turbine